Whispers of an Endless Love

Biswajit Paria

Copyright

Dedication

To my wonderful wife, Payel, and my precious daughter, Titli—your love and support are the heartbeats of my life. This book is for you both, with all my love and gratitude.

Prologue

The wind moved gently through the village of Nagra, carrying with it secrets only the mountains knew. It was a place of quiet beauty, nestled deep in the heart of the hills, where the world seemed to pause and hold its breath. The river that wound through the village whispered softly as it had for centuries, and the ancient trees stood tall, their branches reaching out as if to touch the sky. But beneath the tranquil surface, Nagra was a place haunted by memories—by the echoes of a love that refused to fade.

In the heart of the village, on a worn wooden bench beneath an old tree, sat a man. His face was etched with the passage of time, his eyes clouded by years of longing and sorrow. He was known as the "mad man in love," a title whispered among the villagers with a mixture of pity and reverence. To them, he was a relic of the past, a man trapped in a story that had long since ended.

But for Tarun, the story had never ended. It lingered in the air, woven into the very fabric of the village, a presence that refused to be forgotten. He could still hear her voice, soft and distant, carried on the wind like a melody from another time. He could still feel her touch, a whisper against his skin, as if she had never truly left.

The villagers didn't know, couldn't understand. To them, the past was something to be left behind, a shadow that faded with time. But Tarun knew better. He knew that some loves were too powerful to be erased, too deep to be bound by the limits of life and death. His love had outlived the years, had outlived even her, and now it whispered through the village like the wind, touching everything but never staying long enough to be seen.

As the sun dipped below the horizon and the shadows lengthened, Tarun sat in silence, listening. He waited, as he always did, for the moment when the wind would shift, carrying with it the faintest trace of her presence. And when it came—soft and elusive—he closed his eyes and let the memories wash over him.

"Through every breath, I still feel you near,

The words floated on the air, as they had for years, a melody that only he could hear. It was a song of love, of loss, of promises that had never been fulfilled. And as Tarun listened, he knew that his story was far from over. It lived on in the whispers of the wind, in the quiet rustling of the leaves, in the heart of the village that had become his home.

Chapter 1: Echoes of a Lost Melody

The village of Nagra seemed frozen in time, untouched by the turbulence of the world beyond its borders. Cradled in the arms of the mountains, it offered a sanctuary of quiet beauty—a place where the wind seemed to carry secrets through the ancient trees and the river moved with an almost meditative calm. Visitors came seeking peace, lured by the promise of tranquility, but few realized that beneath the surface, Nagra held stories that whispered of love, loss, and something far deeper.

In the heart of the village square sat an old man, his figure blending with the timelessness of the stone paths beneath his feet. His skin was etched with deep lines, his face worn by the weight of years, and his eyes—clouded yet sharp with memories—seemed to carry a depth of sorrow that no one dared to question. The villagers called him the "mad man in love," a title murmured with a strange mixture of pity and reverence, as if they sensed that his madness was tied to something sacred.

One quiet afternoon, when the sun hung low in the sky and cast a golden hue over the village, a young couple found their way to the square. They had come to Nagra in search of something—peace, perhaps, or a reprieve from the relentless pace of their lives. But as they wandered among the stone buildings and felt the cool mountain air brush against their skin, they sensed something more. It was as if the village itself held its breath, waiting for something to be revealed.

And then they heard it.

A melody, distant yet haunting, floated on the breeze like a memory half-forgotten but never truly lost. The voice that carried it was filled with a sorrow so deep it seemed to seep into the very air around them:

"Through every breath, I still feel you near,
Yet every step I take is shadowed by the tear..."

The couple stopped, exchanging glances, their curiosity piqued. The melody wrapped around them, gentle yet insistent, stirring emotions they couldn't quite name. It was as though the song had always been there, waiting for them to hear it.

They followed the sound, their steps drawn toward its source, until they found themselves standing before the old man on the worn wooden bench. He sat still as stone, his hands resting in his lap, his gaze fixed on the horizon as if searching for something just beyond the edge of sight. The couple hesitated, unsure whether to approach, but there was something about him—an aura of quiet sadness that beckoned them closer, urging them to sit beside him.

The old man, whose name was Tarun, turned slowly to face them. His eyes, though clouded by age, held a depth that startled the young couple. They had expected to see madness in his gaze, but what they saw instead was a life shaped by love and loss, a story etched into every line of his weathered face.

For a long moment, Tarun said nothing, as if weighing whether to speak at all. Then, in a voice that seemed to carry the weight of the mountains themselves, he broke the silence.

"Let me tell you," he began softly, "about a love that was greater than life itself... and the price I paid to hold onto it."

His words hung in the air like the lingering notes of the melody, and the couple felt something shift within them. They had come to Nagra in search of tranquility, but what they had found was far more profound. There was something in the old man's voice—a quiet intensity, a deep reservoir of emotion—that demanded their attention, pulling them into a world they hadn't known they were searching for.

Tarun's gaze drifted past them, to the distant mountains that stood as silent witnesses to his story. His expression was far away, as if he were seeing through the veil of years to a moment long forgotten by the world, but never by him.

The noise of the village square, the rustling of the trees, the warmth of the sun—all of it seemed to fade into the background. The couple leaned in unconsciously, their hearts beating a little faster, as they prepared to be transported into another time, another place. The world around them grew distant, leaving only Tarun's voice and the story that lingered on the edge of his lips.

And so, as the shadows lengthened and the village of Nagra remained suspended in its quiet magic, the old man began to weave a tale—a tale that would change the couple's lives forever.

Chapter 2: The Fateful Train Journey

Tarun leaned back in his seat, a satisfied smile playing on his lips as the train chugged away from the bustling city station. The rhythmic clattering of the wheels against the tracks was a comforting sound, a steady reminder that he was finally on his way to the much-needed vacation he had been dreaming of for weeks. The scent of fresh rain on the tracks mingled with the occasional waft of food from the vendor's cart, adding to the atmosphere of adventure.

The journey to the hill station had been planned meticulously by Tarun and his close-knit group of friends. After months of grueling study sessions and the intense pressure of university exams, this trip was their collective escape—a reward for their hard work and a chance to recharge before the next phase of their lives began.

Tarun's friends occupied the seats around him, their laughter and banter filling the compartment with a sense of camaraderie. Rohan, the group's self-proclaimed leader, was in the midst of recounting one of his many exaggerated tales of heroism, much to the amusement of the others. Beside him, Neha and Akash were engaged in a playful argument over the best spots to visit once they reached the hill station, while Meera, the quietest of the group, was absorbed in a book, her eyes occasionally drifting to the passing scenery outside the window.

Tarun himself was content to simply soak in the moment. The train ride through the mountains promised breathtaking views, and the thought of crisp, cool air and scenic trails filled him with anticipation. As the train wound its way through the city and out into the countryside, Tarun felt a sense of freedom he hadn't experienced in a long time. The weight of exams and deadlines seemed to lift with each passing mile, replaced by the lightness of possibility.

"Hey, Tarun," Rohan called out, snapping Tarun out of his reverie. "You haven't said much since we left. What's on your mind, buddy?"

Tarun grinned, shaking his head. "Nothing much, just enjoying the ride. It's been a while since I could relax like this."

Neha, always perceptive, raised an eyebrow. "You sure you're not thinking about those exams again? Come on, we're on vacation! No more stress, remember?"

Tarun chuckled, waving off her concern. "I'm serious, Neha. I'm just looking forward to the mountains, the fresh air... and maybe a little adventure."

"Adventure, huh?" Akash leaned in, a mischievous glint in his eyes. "I bet you're hoping to find some mysterious old temple or hidden treasure in the hills."

"Or maybe a pretty girl who'll fall for your charms," Rohan teased, earning a round of laughter from the group.

Tarun rolled his eyes good-naturedly. "You guys watch too many movies. I'm just looking forward to some peace and quiet."

Meera, who had been quietly observing the conversation, finally spoke up. "You know, Tarun, the mountains are said to be full of mysteries. Who knows what we might discover?"

Her words, though spoken with a hint of playfulness, carried an undercurrent of something more—a sense of curiosity, perhaps, or a subtle warning. Tarun met her gaze, intrigued by the seriousness in her tone, but before he could ask her to elaborate, the train began to slow down as it approached a small, rural station.

"Looks like we're stopping," Akash noted, glancing out the window. "Must be one of those tiny stations in the middle of nowhere."

The train's whistle echoed through the air as it came to a halt, and the group watched as a handful of passengers disembarked. The station was quiet, with only a few people milling about, and the surrounding landscape was a patchwork of fields and distant hills. The sky, which had been clear earlier, was now overcast, and a cool breeze rustled through the trees, hinting at the changing weather.

"Hope it doesn't rain," Neha murmured, her eyes on the darkening clouds. "That would put a damper on our plans."

"Don't worry," Rohan said confidently. "Even if it does, we'll make the best of it. Nothing can ruin this trip."

As the train resumed its journey, Tarun glanced out the window at the gathering clouds, a sense of unease settling in his chest. He couldn't quite shake the feeling that Meera's words had stirred something within him—a nagging thought that their adventure might turn out to be more than they had bargained for. But he quickly dismissed the feeling, focusing instead on the excitement of the journey ahead. After all, they were young, carefree, and on the brink of a memorable adventure. What could possibly go wrong?

As the train continued its ascent into the mountains, the landscape outside the window transformed into a picturesque scene of rolling hills and dense forests. The air grew cooler, and the scent of pine and earth replaced the urban smells of the city. The passengers, including Tarun and his friends, marveled at the beauty of the surroundings, their earlier worries about the weather temporarily forgotten.

The train wound its way along the narrow tracks, occasionally passing through tunnels that plunged the compartment into darkness before emerging once more into the light. The rhythmic clatter of the wheels against the rails was soothing, and many of the passengers settled into their seats, lulled by the gentle rocking of the train.

But as the afternoon wore on, the sky grew darker, the clouds thickening and casting a somber pall over the landscape. The wind picked up, rustling the leaves of the trees and sending occasional gusts through the open windows. Tarun watched as the first drops of rain splattered against the glass, their gentle patter gradually intensifying into a steady downpour.

"Looks like we spoke too soon," Akash said, frowning as he watched the rain. "This isn't just a passing shower."

Neha sighed, pulling her jacket closer around her shoulders. "I knew it. We're going to be stuck inside when we get there."

"Relax, Neha," Rohan said, trying to lighten the mood. "It's just a little rain. We'll be fine."

But even Rohan's usual optimism couldn't completely dispel the growing sense of unease that settled over the group. The rain, which had started as a light drizzle, was now coming down in sheets, obscuring the view outside and drumming loudly on the roof of the train. The wind howled through the trees, and the temperature seemed to drop with each passing minute.

Tarun felt a knot of anxiety form in his stomach as he stared out at the storm. The mountains, which had seemed so inviting earlier, now loomed dark and foreboding in the distance. The train's pace had slowed considerably, the engine straining against the steep incline and the treacherous weather.

Meera, who had been quiet for most of the journey, suddenly spoke up. "Do you feel that?"

The others turned to her, puzzled. "Feel what?" Tarun asked, though he had a sinking feeling that he knew what she meant.

"The air... it's different," Meera said, her voice barely audible over the noise of the storm. "Heavier. Like something's about to happen."

A shiver ran down Tarun's spine at her words. He had felt it too—a change in the atmosphere, a sense of impending doom that seemed to hang over them like a dark cloud. He glanced around the compartment, noting that many of the other passengers appeared uneasy as well, their faces pale and tense. The train continued its slow, laborious climb up the mountainside, the storm growing more intense with each passing moment. The wind battered the sides of the train, causing it to sway slightly on the tracks. The rain was now coming down in torrents, flooding the narrow mountain roads and turning the landscape into a blur of gray and green.

Tarun's heart began to race as the train approached a sharp curve in the tracks, the old bridge that spanned the river below just visible through the sheets of rain. The bridge, a narrow, rickety structure made of wood and iron, had always been a point of concern for travelers. Its age and the harsh mountain conditions had taken their toll, and many wondered how long it would hold up under the strain. The train's whistle pierced the air as it neared the bridge, a haunting sound that seemed to echo off the mountains. The tension in the compartment was palpable, everyone holding their breath as the train began to cross the bridge.

For a moment, it seemed as though they would make it. The train moved slowly, cautiously, over the rickety structure, the creaking of the wood and the groaning of the metal drowned out by the storm. But just as the last car began to cross, there was a deafening crack—a sound that cut through the noise of the storm like a knife. Tarun felt his heart stop as the bridge gave way beneath them.

Time seemed to slow as the train lurched violently, the front cars tilting dangerously as the bridge collapsed under their weight. Screams filled the air as passengers were thrown from their seats, their belongings tumbling around them in a chaotic mess. Tarun's hands shot out to grip the armrests of his seat, his knuckles white as he struggled to hold on.

The train car shuddered and groaned, metal screeching against metal as it teetered on the edge of the broken bridge. The lights flickered, casting eerie shadows across the faces of the terrified passengers. For a brief, heart-stopping moment, the train hung in the balance, as if deciding whether to plummet into the abyss or cling to the remnants of the bridge. Then, with a sickening lurch, the train began to fall.

Tarun was thrown from his seat as the car tipped forward, the floor becoming the ceiling as gravity took hold. He heard the panicked cries of his friends, the desperate shouts of the other passengers, and the deafening roar of the river below as the train plunged downward. His body slammed against the walls of the compartment, pain exploding in his side as he collided with the hard metal.

The world spun around him in a blur of sound and motion. He could barely make sense of what was happening—one moment he was falling, the next he was tumbling, his vision filled with flashes of rain, metal, and darkness. His head struck something solid, and a sharp pain shot through his skull, blurring his vision and filling his ears with a high-pitched ringing.

In the chaos, Tarun caught a glimpse of Rohan, his face twisted in terror as he clung to a seat, his fingers white from the strain. Neha was screaming, her voice raw with fear, while Akash struggled to reach her, his arms outstretched. Meera, who had been seated across from Tarun, was nowhere to be seen—lost in the maelstrom of bodies and debris that filled the compartment.

The train car crashed into the river with a bone-jarring impact, the force of the collision knocking the breath from Tarun's lungs. Water surged into the compartment, icy and relentless, flooding the floor and rising quickly. Tarun gasped for air, his body battered and bruised, as he struggled to stay afloat in the rapidly filling car.

The sound of the rushing water was deafening, drowning out the cries of the passengers as they fought to escape. The train car was sinking fast, the weight of the water pulling it deeper into the river. Tarun's heart pounded in his chest as he realized the full extent of their peril—if they didn't get out soon, they would all be trapped in the sinking train, dragged down to the bottom of the river.

With a surge of adrenaline, Tarun forced himself to move, pushing through the rising water as he searched for an exit. The compartment was in complete disarray, seats torn from the floor, luggage floating in the murky water, and broken glass glinting in the dim light. Tarun's fingers brushed against a jagged edge, slicing his skin, but he ignored the pain, his only focus on finding a way out.

He spotted a broken window near the rear of the car, the glass shattered and the frame twisted from the impact. The water was already lapping at the edge of the window, the car tilting as it continued to sink.

Tarun's lungs burned with the need for air, his chest tight as he struggled to keep his head above water.

"Over here!" he shouted, his voice hoarse and desperate. "This way!"

His friends, hearing his call, began to fight their way toward him. Rohan was the first to reach the window, his face pale and streaked with blood. He grasped the edge of the frame, pulling himself up with trembling arms, his breath coming in ragged gasps. Neha and Akash followed, their movements sluggish and frantic as they battled the rising water.

Tarun pushed them forward, urging them through the narrow opening one by one. Rohan went first, squeezing through the broken window and disappearing into the dark waters outside. Neha was next, her eyes wide with fear as she hesitated for just a moment before following Rohan. Akash gave Tarun a grim nod before climbing through the window, his expression one of determination and dread.

But as Tarun turned to help Meera, he realized with a jolt of terror that she was nowhere to be found. Panic seized him, his heart racing as he scanned the waterlogged compartment for any sign of her. The water was nearly up to his chest now, cold and unforgiving, and the train car was tilting at a dangerous angle.

"Meera!" Tarun shouted, his voice cracking with desperation. "Meera, where are you?"

There was no response, only the roar of the water and the creaking of the sinking train. Tarun's mind raced as he tried to think of where she could be—trapped under a seat, caught in the debris, or worse, already lost to the dark depths of the river.

Just as he was about to dive into the water to search for her, a hand shot out from beneath the surface, grasping wildly at the air. Tarun lunged forward, grabbing the hand and pulling with all his strength. Meera's head broke the surface, her face pale and her eyes wide with terror as she gasped for air.

"Tarun!" she choked, her voice barely audible above the noise. "Help me!"

Tarun didn't hesitate. He wrapped his arms around her, pulling her toward the broken window as the water continued to rise around them. Meera was weak, her movements sluggish and uncoordinated, but she clung to him with a desperate strength, her fear giving her the will to keep fighting. Together, they reached the window, but the opening was barely wide enough for one person to fit through at a time. Tarun pushed Meera forward, guiding her hands to the edge of the frame and helping her pull herself up. The water was up to his shoulders now, the weight of it dragging him down as he tried to keep Meera afloat.

"You go first," Tarun urged, his voice strained. "I'll follow right behind you."

Meera hesitated, her eyes filled with fear and uncertainty. "But what about you?"

"I'll be fine," Tarun assured her, though he wasn't entirely sure of that himself. "Just go. Please."

With a final, terrified look, Meera squeezed through the window, disappearing into the dark waters outside. Tarun watched her go, his heart pounding in his chest as he prepared to follow. But as he moved to pull himself up, the train car lurched violently, the water surging around him as the car tilted even further. Tarun's grip slipped, and he was pulled under the water, his head striking something solid as he was thrown backward. Pain exploded in his skull, and his vision went black, the world around him fading into nothingness as he lost consciousness.

Tarun awoke to the sound of distant voices, his body cold and aching all over. His head throbbed with pain, and his lungs burned with the remnants of water he had inhaled. For a moment, he was disoriented, unsure of where he was or how he had survived. As his vision cleared, he realized he was lying on a rocky riverbank, the night sky above him dotted with stars. The storm had passed, leaving the air cool and still, the only sound the gentle lapping of the river against the shore. Tarun blinked up at the sky, trying to make sense of what had happened. He remembered the train, the bridge, the fall into the river... and then nothing. How had he ended up here? And where were his friends?

Tarun tried to sit up, but a sharp pain in his side forced him back down. He winced, clutching his ribs as he took stock of his injuries. His clothes were soaked and torn, his skin bruised and scraped, but he was alive. Somehow, he had survived the fall and the river's icy grip.

But what about the others? The thought sent a jolt of fear through him, and he forced himself to sit up, ignoring the pain. His eyes scanned the riverbank, searching for any sign of his friends. The darkness made it difficult to see, but he could just make out the shapes of several figures lying nearby, their bodies motionless.

Exhausted and heartbroken, Tarun finally collapsed on the riverbank, his body and spirit battered by the events of the night. The reality of his situation was sinking in—he was alone in the wilderness, far from help, and he had lost everything. The night stretched on, cold and unforgiving, as he huddled for warmth and comfort. The storm had passed, but its aftermath had left him shattered, his once-bright spirits dimmed by loss and fear.

Tarun stared up at the sky, the stars distant and indifferent to his suffering. He couldn't shake the feeling that this was only the beginning of his ordeal—that the true horrors of the night were yet to come.

But for now, all he could do was cling to the hope that he would survive the night and somehow find his way back to safety. And as he drifted into a fitful sleep, the last thing he saw was the cold, dark river, its waters flowing silently toward an unknown destination.

Chapter 3: Recovery in Nagra and Growing Affection

Nagra was a place where time seemed to slow, as if the rest of the world had forgotten about this remote village nestled deep within the mountains. The landscape was both breathtaking and ominous—massive peaks loomed in every direction, their jagged edges cutting into the sky. Thick forests stretched as far as the eye could see, the trees ancient and imposing, their trunks twisted by centuries of harsh winds and snow. The village itself sat in a secluded valley, surrounded by natural barriers that made it nearly impossible to reach. It was as if Nagra had been deliberately hidden from the world, tucked away in a secret fold of the earth.

It was here, along the banks of a raging river, that Tarun had been found.

The storm had passed, leaving behind a landscape scarred by nature's fury. The river that had once been a tranquil stream had transformed into a torrent of icy water, swollen by the rains and churning with debris. It was in this tumultuous current that the villagers of Nagra had discovered Tarun, his body battered and barely alive, washed up on the rocky shore like driftwood.

The men who found him were weathered by the elements, their faces hardened by years of living in this unforgiving landscape. They moved with quiet efficiency, their strong hands lifting Tarun's limp form from the riverbank. There was no hesitation in their actions, no need for words. They knew what needed to be done.

Tarun's unconscious body was carried through the winding paths of Nagra, past stone houses with thatched roofs and narrow alleyways that twisted like a labyrinth. The village was quiet, the only sounds the wind rustling through the trees and the distant roar of the river. The men brought him to the village leader's home, a modest structure at the far end of the village, where the air was thick with the scent of herbs and smoke from the ever-burning fire.

The village leader, an elderly man named Shankar, took Tarun into his care. Shankar was a man of few words, but his eyes held a quiet wisdom, and his hands were skilled in the ways of healing. He had seen many injuries in his time—both from the harshness of the mountains and from the secrets that lay buried beneath Nagra's serene surface.

For days, Tarun drifted in and out of consciousness, his mind foggy with pain and fevered dreams. Each time he awoke, he found himself in the same small room, with rough stone walls and a single window that looked out onto the towering mountains. The fire in the hearth burned steadily, providing warmth against the chill that seemed to permeate the very air of the village.

Shankar was always nearby, offering water and broth in small doses, his presence a constant source of calm. He rarely spoke, but his hands moved with the practiced ease of someone who had spent a lifetime caring for others. Under Shankar's watchful eye, Tarun's strength slowly returned, though the memories of the storm and the river still haunted his dreams.

It was during one of these moments of wakefulness that Tarun first began to notice the oddities in Nagra. The villagers who came and went from Shankar's home were always polite, but there was a distance to them, a guardedness that Tarun couldn't quite place. They avoided meeting his eyes, their conversations stilted and cautious, as if they were hiding something just beneath the surface.

As Tarun's health improved, so did his curiosity. He began to explore the village in small doses, first with the help of a cane and then on his own, his body still weak but his mind growing sharper with each passing day. The village of Nagra was beautiful in its simplicity—stone houses built to withstand the harsh winters, narrow paths that wound between homes like veins in the earth, and the ever-present mountains that loomed over everything like silent sentinels.

But there was something else, something that lingered in the air like a shadow. The villagers were too quiet, too reserved. Even the children seemed subdued, their laughter stifled as if by an unseen force. Tarun could feel it—an undercurrent of fear and tension that ran through the village, unspoken but always present. It was as if everyone in Nagra was carrying a secret, something they were too afraid to share.

Tarun's curiosity grew with each passing day, and he found himself compelled to uncover the truth. What were the villagers hiding? Why did they avoid speaking of the past? And why did he feel as if he was being watched, even when he was alone?

It was during one of his walks through the village that he met Priya, the village leader's daughter.

She was unlike anyone Tarun had ever met—beautiful, intelligent, and with an air of quiet strength that seemed to radiate from her every movement. She was younger than he had expected, in her early twenties, with dark eyes that seemed to hold the weight of the world. Her long hair was tied back in a loose braid, and she wore a simple sari that did nothing to hide her natural grace. There was something about her that drew him in, something he couldn't quite explain.

Priya worked as a schoolteacher, responsible for the education of the village children, but there was a depth to her that went far beyond her role as an educator. She moved through the village with purpose, her eyes always watching, always observing. Tarun couldn't help but notice how the villagers seemed to respect her, how they deferred to her in a way that went beyond her being the village leader's daughter.

Their first meeting was brief. Priya had come to check on him at her father's request, her hands gentle as she adjusted his bandages and made sure he was comfortable. She was polite but distant, her words carefully chosen and her gaze always averted.

"You're recovering well," she said softly, her voice as soothing as the wind through the trees. "But you should be careful not to overexert yourself. The mountains are unforgiving."

Tarun nodded, grateful for her care but still wary. There was something in her eyes, something that hinted at a deeper story—a story she wasn't ready to share. He wanted to ask her about the village, about the secrets he could feel lurking just beneath the surface, but he knew that pushing too hard would only make her retreat further.

As the days passed, Priya continued to visit him regularly. Their conversations were brief at first, filled with small talk and pleasantries, but as Tarun's health improved, so did their interactions. He found himself drawn to her, not just because of her beauty but because of the way she carried herself—with grace and quiet determination. There was a sadness in her eyes, a burden she bore silently, and Tarun couldn't help but wonder what secrets she was hiding.

One evening, as the sun dipped low behind the mountains, casting the village in a warm golden light, Tarun and Priya found themselves sitting together by the river that had become his refuge. The water flowed steadily over the rocks, its sound a soothing melody that eased the tension in Tarun's chest. The village around them was quiet, the air still and cool as the day faded into night.

Tarun glanced at Priya, who sat beside him with her gaze fixed on the water. She looked peaceful, but he could see the tension in her posture, the way her fingers gripped the edge of the stone she was sitting on. He wanted to ask her what was wrong, wanted to know what was weighing on her mind, but he wasn't sure if she would tell him.

"Priya," he began cautiously, his voice low, "there's something about this village... something that doesn't feel right. Everyone seems to be hiding something."

Priya stiffened at his words, her eyes flicking toward him for a brief moment before she quickly looked away. She remained silent for a long time, the only sound the rush of the river and the distant calls of birds returning to their nests.

Finally, she spoke, her voice quiet and careful. "Nagra... is not like other villages. There are things here... things that are better left unspoken."

Tarun frowned, his concern growing. "What do you mean? What are you trying to tell me?"

Priya turned to face him then, her dark eyes filled with an emotion he couldn't quite place. It was a mixture of fear, sadness, and something else—something that looked a lot like affection. She hesitated for a moment, as if weighing her words carefully, before she spoke again.

"Tarun," she whispered, her voice trembling slightly, "I can't tell you everything. There are secrets in this village that... that are dangerous. It's safer if you don't ask too many questions."

Tarun's heart skipped a beat at her words. He could see the fear in her eyes, the conflict that tore at her from within. He reached out and gently took her hand, the warmth of her skin a small comfort against the cold truth of her warning.

"Priya," he said softly, his voice filled with concern, "whatever it is, you don't have to face it alone. I'm here. I want to help."

Priya's grip on his hand tightened for a brief moment before she pulled away, her expression conflicted. She looked down at their hands for a long time, as if trying to memorize the feel of his touch, before she finally met his gaze again.

Tarun's concern for her only grew with each passing day. He wanted to protect her, to shield her from whatever danger was lurking in the shadows of Nagra. But he also knew that she was stronger than she appeared.

Their connection grew stronger with each passing day. Tarun found himself falling for her, drawn to her quiet strength and the depth of her emotions. And Priya, despite her best efforts to remain detached, found herself caring for him more than she had ever intended.

At first, she had tried to keep her distance, to treat him like any other outsider who had stumbled into the village. But there was something about him—something in the way he looked at her, the way he spoke to her, that made it impossible for her to remain indifferent. His kindness, his concern for her, had slowly worn away the walls she had built around herself, leaving her vulnerable in a way she hadn't been in years.

She had never intended to fall in love. It was dangerous, foolish even, given her position. But love had a way of creeping in, of finding the cracks in even the most carefully constructed defenses. And now, she had grown to love Tarun, and that love had made her weak.

The days passed, and Tarun's strength continued to return. He spent more time outside, exploring the village and its surroundings, always with Priya by his side. The bond between them deepened, unspoken words passing between them in the quiet moments they shared.

Nagra, with its stone paths and simple houses, was beautiful in its own way, but there was always an undercurrent of unease that Tarun couldn't shake. The villagers were kind, but they were distant, their smiles never quite reaching their eyes. It was as if they were all living under a shadow, and no one dared to speak of the darkness that loomed over them.

One evening, as the sun set behind the mountains, casting the village in a warm golden light, Tarun and Priya found themselves sitting by the river. The water flowed steadily over the rocks, its sound a soothing melody that eased the tension in Tarun's chest.

Priya sat beside him, her gaze fixed on the water, her thoughts clearly elsewhere. Tarun reached out and gently touched her hand, bringing her back to the present. He simply held her hand, offering her the only comfort he could. They sat together in the fading light, their hearts connected by an unspoken understanding.

But as the shadows grew longer and the night began to settle over the village, she let herself stay in that moment with Tarun, their hands entwined, their hearts beating in sync. But the darkness was closing in, and she knew that the peace they had found would not last forever.

Chapter 4: The Ghost of Nagra's Secrets

The village of Nagra, with its quiet streets and stone houses, continued to hold its secrets close. Tarun's recovery had been slow but steady, and as his strength returned, so did his curiosity. He couldn't shake the feeling that something was terribly wrong in the village—something the villagers were too afraid to speak about. The quiet, the subdued nature of the people, the distant look in their eyes—it all pointed to a truth buried beneath the surface, waiting to be uncovered.

It was this need to understand, this burning desire to know the truth, that drove Tarun to explore the village more deeply. He walked the narrow stone paths, his steps deliberate, his eyes scanning every detail of the place that had both saved his life and now seemed to suffocate him with its unspoken mysteries. The villagers greeted him politely enough, but there was always a distance in their interactions, as if they were wary of getting too close.

One afternoon, as the sun hung low in the sky, casting long shadows across the village, Tarun found himself wandering near the outskirts of Nagra. The houses here were older, more worn by time and the elements. The streets were quieter, the air thick with the scent of pine and earth. It was here that he met Ravi, an elderly man with a hunched back and deep lines etched into his weathered face.

Ravi was sitting on a small wooden bench outside his modest home, his gaze distant as if lost in memories of a time long past. He barely noticed Tarun's approach until the younger man was standing right in front of him.

"Good afternoon," Tarun said, his voice gentle so as not to startle the old man.

Ravi blinked and looked up at him, his eyes cloudy with age. There was a sadness in his expression, a heaviness that weighed on his shoulders. He nodded in response but said nothing, his gaze returning to the horizon as if searching for something that had long since disappeared.

Tarun hesitated for a moment before sitting down beside him on the bench. The silence between them stretched out, but it wasn't uncomfortable. In fact, there was something peaceful about it, as if they were both waiting for the right moment to speak.

"I've been staying in the village leader's home," Tarun said after a long pause, his voice quiet. "I was found by the river after the storm. They saved my life."

Ravi nodded again, still not looking at him. "Shankar is a good man," he said, his voice rough and raspy. "He's done what he can for this village... but there are some things even he can't stop."

Tarun felt a chill run down his spine at the old man's words. "What do you mean?" he asked, leaning forward slightly.

Ravi sighed, the sound heavy with years of burden. He finally turned to look at Tarun, his eyes filled with a sorrow that spoke of untold pain. "There are dark secrets in this village, young man. Secrets that have been buried for far too long. And the longer they stay buried, the more they rot... until they poison everything around them."

Tarun's heart raced. This was the first time anyone had spoken so openly about the village's secrets. "What kind of secrets?" he asked, his voice barely above a whisper.

Ravi glanced around, as if checking to make sure no one was listening. He leaned in closer, his voice low and conspiratorial. "I used to work at the old railway station," he said. "Back when the government first came to this village. They said they were here to help us, to bring progress and development... but that was just a lie."

Tarun listened intently, his pulse quickening. "What were they really doing?"

Ravi's expression darkened. "They were running experiments. Something called the Mind-Wave project. They never told us exactly what it was, but it didn't take long for us to figure out that we were the subjects of their tests. They used us—our minds, our bodies—for their experiments, and when they were done with us, they moved on to another location. But the damage was already done."

Tarun's stomach twisted with unease. "What kind of damage?"

Ravi looked down at his hands, his fingers trembling slightly. "The villagers... they were left to suffer the consequences. Our health started to deteriorate—slowly at first, but it got worse over time. Some of us started losing our memories, others became paranoid, afraid of shadows that weren't really there. And then... people started disappearing. No one ever talked about it, but we all knew. If you got too close to the truth, you vanished."

Tarun felt a knot tighten in his chest. The fear in Ravi's voice was palpable, and it only made the sense of dread that had been building in him grow stronger. "Is that why the village is so quiet? Why everyone seems so... afraid?"

Ravi nodded, his eyes filled with a lifetime of regret. "We're afraid because we know what happens when you push too hard. The government may not be here anymore, but their shadow still lingers over us. We're always being watched, always being monitored... and no one dares to speak out."

Tarun was silent for a moment, processing everything Ravi had told him. The Mind-Wave project... it sounded like something out of a nightmare, something that shouldn't exist in the real world. But here, in Nagra, it was very real, and its effects were still being felt.

"There's something else," Ravi said suddenly, his voice dropping to a whisper. "Something you need to know."

Tarun leaned in closer, his heart pounding in his chest. "What is it?"

Ravi's gaze grew distant, his eyes clouded with fear. "There's a train," he said, his voice barely audible. "A train that comes in the dead of night. It never stops for passengers. No one boards. No one leaves. But when it arrives... the air changes. You can feel it—your heart races, your mind... slips away. And those who see it... they're never the same."

Tarun felt a cold shiver run down his spine. The train... it was a phantom that haunted the village, a symbol of everything that was wrong in Nagra. He had heard whispers of it before, but no one had ever spoken of it so directly. Could it be connected to the Mind-Wave project? Was it still part of the government's experiments, even after all these years?

Ravi seemed to sense Tarun's thoughts. "The train is part of it," he said, his voice trembling. "It's all connected. The experiments, the disappearances... they're all tied to that train. I don't know how, but I know it's true. And if you see it... if you get too close... you'll never be the same."

Tarun swallowed hard, his mind racing with questions. He wanted to know more, needed to understand what was happening in this village, but Ravi's fear was infectious, and he couldn't shake the feeling that he was treading dangerously close to something he wasn't meant to uncover.

"Why are you telling me this?" Tarun asked, his voice shaky.

Ravi looked at him, his expression weary but resolute. "Because I'm dying," he said simply. "I don't have much time left, and I can't take these secrets to my grave. The government has hurt us enough... and someone needs to stop them."

Tarun felt a surge of determination rise within him. He had come to Nagra by accident, but now he knew that he couldn't leave without getting to the bottom of the village's dark secrets. He owed it to Ravi, to the villagers who had suffered in silence for so long, to find out the truth.

As they sat in silence, a sound echoed in the distance—a faint rumble, like the low growl of thunder. Tarun's breath caught in his throat as he turned toward the source of the sound, his eyes narrowing against the dim light.

And then he saw it—a figure standing near the old railway tracks, barely visible against the darkening sky. It was a woman, her silhouette outlined by the fading light. She stood still for a moment, watching them, before quietly slipping away into the shadows.

"Who was that?" Tarun asked, his voice hushed.

Ravi didn't respond, his gaze fixed on the spot where the woman had stood. His face was pale, his hands trembling.

Tarun felt a sense of unease settle over him. The woman's presence felt wrong, like she was a part of the village's dark history, a ghost of the past that had returned to haunt them. He wanted to go after her, to find out who she was and what she knew, but something held him back—a deep, instinctual fear that told him to stay away.

The sun dipped below the horizon, casting the village in shadow. The air grew colder, the sky darkening into night. Tarun stood up, his mind racing with everything Ravi had told him. He knew that he couldn't stay silent any longer. He had to find out the truth, no matter the cost.

Later that night, as Tarun sat by the fire in the village leader's home, his mind was still buzzing with the conversation he had had with Ravi. The old man's words echoed in his head, filling him with a sense of urgency and dread. The Mind-Wave project, the mysterious train, the disappearances... it was all connected, and he was determined to uncover the truth.

But as he stared into the flames, lost in thought, he heard the soft sound of footsteps approaching. He looked up to see Priya standing in the doorway, her expression tense. There was a hesitancy in her movements, a nervousness that hadn't been there before.

"Tarun," she said quietly, stepping into the room. "Can we talk?"

Tarun nodded, motioning for her to sit beside him. Priya moved to the fire, her gaze fixed on the flames as she sat down on the small wooden bench beside him. For a long moment, neither of them spoke, the crackling of the fire the only sound between them.

Priya's gaze remained on the fire, her expression conflicted. "There are things in this village that you shouldn't be involved in, Tarun. Things that are dangerous... and the more you dig, the more you'll put yourself in harm's way."

Tarun's heart raced at her words. "What are you trying to say, Priya?"

She finally turned to look at him, her eyes filled with a mixture of fear and affection. "I'm saying that you should stop asking questions. Stop trying to find out what's going on here. It's safer that way... for both of us."

Tarun's heart ached at the pain in her voice, but he knew that he couldn't turn back now. He was too deep into the mystery, too invested in finding out the truth. He couldn't just walk away, not when so much was at stake.

"I can't do that, Priya," he said quietly. "I need to know the truth."

With that, she hurried out of the room, leaving Tarun alone by the fire. He watched her go, his heart heavy with both love and frustration. He knew that Priya was trying to protect him, trying to keep him from getting too close to the darkness that haunted Nagra. But he also knew that he couldn't stop now. He had to find out the truth, no matter the cost.

Chapter 5: The Secret Beneath the Ruins

The morning light filtered through the mist that clung to the mountains around Nagra, casting long shadows across the village as the sun rose. Tarun had barely slept the night before, his mind racing with thoughts of what Ravi had revealed to him. The Mind-Wave project, the phantom train, the disappearances—everything was connected, and he was determined to find the truth. The abandoned railway station held the key to uncovering the secrets that had haunted the village for so long.

As Tarun stood at the edge of the village, staring out toward the crumbling ruin that was once the hub of government operations in Nagra, he made up his mind. He would go to the station, search for any clue, and find evidence of the Mind-Wave project and whatever else the government had left behind. The answers were there, waiting to be found, and he couldn't leave without uncovering them.

He left the village leader's home early, slipping out before the village had fully awoken. The air was cool, with a slight breeze that rustled the leaves in the trees. Tarun pulled his jacket tighter around him as he walked, his footsteps echoing on the stone paths. He couldn't shake the feeling that he was being watched, as though unseen eyes were following his every move. The hairs on the back of his neck stood on end, and he found himself glancing over his shoulder more than once, but there was no one there—only the stillness of the morning.

The path to the railway station was overgrown with weeds and brambles, the remnants of what had once been a well-traveled road now nearly swallowed by nature. As Tarun approached the station, the building loomed before him, a decaying monument to the past. Its walls were covered in moss and ivy, the stone crumbling in places where the elements had taken their toll. The roof sagged dangerously, with large sections missing, allowing beams of sunlight to pierce through the darkness inside. The windows were shattered, and the doors hung off their hinges, creaking ominously in the breeze.

Tarun hesitated for a moment at the entrance, his heart pounding in his chest. He knew that whatever he found here could change everything. The Mind-Wave project had left its mark on the village, and he was about to uncover the evidence that could finally bring the truth to light. But the weight of that responsibility pressed down on him, filling him with both fear and determination.

Taking a deep breath, Tarun stepped into the building, the floorboards creaking beneath his feet. Dust motes danced in the beams of light that filtered through the broken windows, and the air was thick with the smell of mildew and decay. The station was eerily silent, save for the occasional drip of water from a leaky roof and the soft rustle of leaves outside.

Tarun moved cautiously through the building, his eyes scanning every corner for anything that might be a clue. He knew that the government had once used this place as a base of operations for the Mind-Wave project, but they had abandoned it long ago, leaving behind only ruins. Still, he hoped that something had been overlooked, something that would reveal the truth.

He began rummaging through the remnants of the station's interior, overturning old furniture and pulling open dusty drawers. Papers and documents lay scattered across the floor, most of them too faded and brittle to be of any use. Broken equipment, rusted beyond recognition, was piled in the corners, their purpose lost to time. Tarun's frustration grew with each dead end, but he refused to give up. He knew that the answer had to be here, somewhere.

As he made his way deeper into the building, Tarun's search became more desperate. He tore through the old filing cabinets, flipped over tables, and pried open lockers, his hands growing filthy with dirt and dust. The minutes ticked by, and still, he found nothing of significance. He could feel his hope slipping away, replaced by a growing sense of dread.

And then, as he was about to give up, something caught his eye—a small, ornate box tucked away in the back of a forgotten cabinet. It was old, covered in a layer of grime, but still intact. Tarun's heart raced as he carefully opened the box, half expecting it to be empty.

But inside, nestled in a bed of faded velvet, was a pocket watch.

At first glance, it appeared to be nothing more than an old timepiece, its surface tarnished with age. But as Tarun picked it up, he felt a strange hum beneath his fingers—a low, almost imperceptible vibration that sent a shiver down his spine. The watch's soft ticking seemed louder than it should have been in the silence of the station, like the heartbeat of something long forgotten.

Tarun's hand trembled as he examined the watch more closely. There was something odd about it, something that didn't quite fit. He carefully turned it over, his fingers tracing the intricate engravings on its surface. It looked like a simple relic of the past, but the way it hummed with that strange frequency told him otherwise.

This wasn't just a watch.

It was a transmitter.

Tarun's breath caught in his throat as the realization hit him. The watch wasn't just an ordinary timepiece—it was a piece of technology, something designed to manipulate the Mind-Wave experiments. Hidden within its delicate mechanisms was a transmitter, a device capable of controlling and enhancing the effects of the project on the villagers.

This was what the government had left behind.

Tarun's mind raced as he pieced together the implications of his discovery. The watch wasn't just a relic; it was a key—a tool once used by high-ranking officials to test the Mind-Wave signals. It was designed to control the frequency of the experiments, to manipulate the minds of the villagers and harness their thoughts for the government's purposes.

As Tarun carefully opened the back of the watch, he found a small compartment hidden within its casing. Inside were tiny microchips, their circuits still intact despite the years of neglect. Along with the microchips were several folded pieces of paper, yellowed with age but still legible.

Tarun unfolded the papers, his eyes scanning the faded writing. They contained coordinates and schematics—blueprints of underground facilities scattered throughout the village. These were the nerve centers of the Mind-Wave project, the places where the experiments had been monitored and controlled.

But the more Tarun read, the more horrifying the truth became. The government hadn't just been experimenting on the villagers for the sake of science—they had been using their minds as a collective supercomputer, harnessing their thoughts for advanced military operations. The villagers had been nothing more than pawns in a game they didn't even know they were playing.

Tarun's stomach churned with anger and disgust as he stared at the papers in his hands. The government had turned Nagra into a living nightmare, a place where the people's very minds were used against them. And now, he had the evidence to prove it.

He quickly folded the papers and slipped them into his pocket, along with the watch. He had seen enough—now he needed to get out of the station and back to Priya. She needed to know what he had found.

As Tarun made his way back through the station, his mind raced with plans. The schematics in the papers showed the locations of the underground facilities—the places where the Mind-Wave project was still being controlled. If he and Priya could find those facilities, they could destroy the project once and for all. They could free the villagers from the government's grip and put an end to the experiments that had haunted Nagra for so long.

But as Tarun stepped out into the daylight, he couldn't shake the feeling that he was being watched. He glanced over his shoulder, his eyes scanning the treeline for any sign of movement. The village seemed quiet, peaceful even, but Tarun knew better. He had learned that nothing in Nagra was ever as it seemed.

He quickened his pace, his heart pounding in his chest as he hurried back to the village leader's home. The sooner he got there, the sooner he could share his discovery with Priya. They had to act fast—there was no telling how much time they had before the government caught wind of their plans.

When Tarun finally arrived at the village leader's home, he found Priya sitting by the fire, her face illuminated by the soft glow of the flames. She looked up as he entered, her eyes widening with concern as she saw the urgency in his expression.

"Tarun, what happened?" she asked, standing up and moving toward him.

Tarun didn't waste any time. He reached into his pocket and pulled out the watch, holding it up for her to see. "I found this at the old railway station," he said, his voice low and serious. "It's not just a watch, Priya. It's a transmitter—part of the Mind-Wave project."

Priya's eyes widened as she took the watch from him, her fingers brushing against the surface as she examined it. "A transmitter?" she whispered, her voice filled with disbelief. "This... this was used to control the experiments?"

Tarun nodded, pulling the folded papers from his pocket and handing them to her. "These papers were with it. They show the locations of underground facilities scattered throughout the village. These are the places where the project is still being controlled. If we can find them, we can destroy the project and save the villagers."

Priya's hands trembled as she unfolded the papers, her eyes scanning the schematics. For a moment, she was silent, her mind racing with the implications of what Tarun had found. And then, slowly, a sense of determination settled over her.

"This... this changes everything," she said, her voice steady despite the weight of her words. "We can't let the government continue doing this to the villagers. We have to find these facilities and shut them down."

Tarun nodded, relief washing over him as he saw the resolve in her eyes. "We'll do it together," he said. "We'll find the control centers and destroy them."

Priya looked up at him, her eyes filled with a mixture of fear and hope. "You're right," she said softly. "But we have to be careful, Tarun. The government has eyes everywhere... and they won't let us stop them without a fight."

Tarun reached out and took her hand, squeezing it gently. "We'll be careful," he promised. "But we can't let them win."

For the first time since they had started working together, Priya allowed herself to believe that they could succeed. She had spent so long keeping her secrets, so long protecting herself from the dangers that lurked in the shadows of Nagra, but now... now she had something worth fighting for. She had Tarun, and she had the villagers who deserved to be free from the nightmare that had been forced upon them.

Over the next few days, Priya and Tarun worked in secret, carefully planning their next move. She even managed to obtain a detailed map of the underground facilities, showing the entrances and exits, the security measures in place, and the locations of the control centers.

When she finally showed the map to Tarun, there was a spark of excitement in her eyes—an excitement born of the possibility that they could actually pull this off.

"This is it," she said, her voice filled with a newfound determination. "We know where the control centers are. Now all we have to do is figure out how to get in... and how to destroy them."

Tarun studied the map, his mind racing with ideas. "We'll need to be smart about this," he said. "We can't just rush in. We need to disable the security systems, take out the guards... and then we can destroy the control centers."

Priya nodded, her gaze steady. "I'll help you every step of the way," she said. "We'll save the village, Tarun. I promise."

For the first time in a long while, Tarun felt a glimmer of hope. They had a plan, they had each other, and they had the will to fight back. Together, they would uncover the truth, dismantle the Mind-Wave project, and free the villagers from the horrors that had plagued them for so long.

But as they prepared for the battle ahead, Tarun couldn't shake the feeling that they were being watched—that the government's eyes were still on them, waiting for the moment to strike.

And in the shadows of Nagra, something dark was stirring.

Chapter 6: Into the Jaws of the Beast

Priya's heart pounded in her chest as she led Tarun through the shadowed outskirts of Nagra. The map she had studied so meticulously was etched in her mind, each detail carefully memorized. She knew where they needed to go, but that didn't make the journey any less perilous. The terrain ahead was treacherous—steep hills, narrow paths, and dense undergrowth that hid the dangers lurking in the darkness. Every step was a gamble, every shadow a potential threat.

The cold mountain air bit at her skin, and the only sounds were the rustling of leaves and the distant cry of night birds. The village of Nagra lay behind them, but the weight of its secrets and fears pressed heavily on her shoulders. She had promised Tarun that she would help him uncover the truth, but now, as they ventured deeper into the unknown, doubt crept into her mind.

Tarun followed her without hesitation. He trusted her, believed in her, and that only made Priya's guilt grow heavier. She knew these mountains, knew the hidden routes and dangerous paths that the villagers avoided. But she also knew the stakes—they were heading toward the heart of the government's operation, a place where danger waited for them in every shadow.

The terrain became more difficult as they climbed higher into the mountains. The narrow path wound between jagged rocks, the ground uneven and slick with moisture from the recent rains. Branches clawed at their clothes, and the air grew colder with every step. Priya moved with purpose, her eyes constantly scanning the surroundings for any sign of movement. She had walked these paths many times before, but tonight felt different. Tonight, the mountains seemed to be holding their breath, waiting for something to happen.

Tarun moved quietly behind her, his footsteps careful on the rocky ground. He trusted her to lead the way, trusted her to know the safest routes through the treacherous landscape. But even as he followed her, his instincts flared. The air was thick with tension, and something felt off.

"Priya," he whispered, his voice barely audible over the sound of the wind. "Are you sure we're on the right path?"

Priya glanced back at him, her eyes filled with both determination and uncertainty. "We're close," she replied, her voice steady. "Just a little further."

But as they approached the location marked on the map—a dilapidated warehouse hidden deep within the forest—Tarun's instincts screamed at him that something was wrong. The building loomed before them, its walls crumbling and covered in moss, its windows shattered and dark. The air felt heavy, oppressive, as if the very ground beneath their feet was holding some dark secret.

Tarun slowed his pace, his senses on high alert. He scanned the area, his eyes searching the shadows for any sign of danger. The hairs on the back of his neck stood on end, and a knot of unease tightened in his chest.

"Wait," he said quietly, reaching out to stop Priya. "Something's not right."

But it was too late.

Figures emerged from the shadows, moving with the precision and silence of trained operatives. They stepped into the faint light filtering through the trees, their faces cold and unreadable. Government officials. Tarun's heart raced as he recognized the dark uniforms, the gleaming weapons at their sides.

"Run!" Tarun hissed to Priya, but before either of them could move, the officials closed in.

A fierce struggle broke out, chaos erupting in the stillness of the night. Tarun fought desperately against overwhelming odds, his muscles straining as he grappled with the nearest official. He was strong, his determination fueled by the need to protect Priya and stop the horrors of the Mind-Wave project, but the numbers were against him. The officials moved with practiced efficiency, their attacks precise and unrelenting.

Tarun lashed out, landing a blow to one of the officials' faces, but another grabbed him from behind, locking his arms in a vice-like grip. He twisted and turned, trying to break free, but more officials rushed in, surrounding him. He could feel his strength waning, his breaths coming in ragged gasps as he struggled to stay on his feet.

In the midst of the chaos, Tarun's mind raced. He knew he couldn't win this fight—not with so many against him. But there was one thing he could still do: protect Priya. With a final surge of strength, he pushed one of the officials away and turned to Priya.

"Go!" he shouted, his voice raw with desperation. "Get out of here!"

Priya's eyes widened with fear, but she hesitated, her heart torn between staying to help Tarun and running to save herself. She couldn't leave him—not like this. But Tarun's fierce gaze told her everything she needed to know. If she stayed, they would both be captured. If she ran, there was a chance she could find a way to save him later.

With tears in her eyes, Priya nodded and turned to flee, her footsteps echoing in the night as she disappeared into the trees. The sound of her own heartbeat pounded in her ears, mingling with the cries of the officials and the sounds of the struggle behind her. She ran blindly through the forest, her mind a whirlwind of fear and guilt.

Tarun's voice echoed in her mind, urging her to keep running, to get away. But with every step she took, her heart shattered a little more. She had left him behind—left him to fight alone. And now he was in the hands of the very people they had been trying to stop.

Priya didn't know how far she had run before she finally stopped, her chest heaving as she leaned against a tree for support. She couldn't hear the sounds of the struggle anymore—only the deafening silence of the forest and the heavy thud of her own heartbeat. Tears blurred her vision as she gasped for breath, her mind racing with thoughts of Tarun.

What had she done? She had promised to protect him, to help him uncover the truth, and now he was gone. Captured. She had delivered him into the jaws of a beast that would not let him go.

Her legs trembled as she forced herself to keep moving, to keep running.

Back in the village, Priya stumbled into her home, her body shaking with exhaustion and fear. The small house felt unbearably empty without Tarun, the silence oppressive as she collapsed onto a chair. She buried her face in her hands, her tears finally spilling over as the weight of what had happened crashed down on her.

She had failed him.

Chapter 7: The Price of Love

The cold night air seeped through the cracks in the walls, wrapping around Priya like a suffocating shroud. She sat by the hearth, her hands clasped tightly together, her mind consumed by thoughts of Tarun. The fire had long since died out, leaving only a faint trace of warmth in the small room, but Priya didn't move to relight it. She barely noticed the chill in the air. All she could feel was the guilt gnawing at her insides, twisting her heart with every sob that escaped her throat.

She had led him to that place. She had brought him straight into the hands of the government. And now he was gone—captured by the very people they had been fighting against. The image of Tarun being dragged away, surrounded by faceless officials, haunted her. She didn't know where they had taken him, didn't know if he was even still alive. The uncertainty gnawed at her, tearing at the fragile hope she had once clung to.

The thought of never seeing him again, of never hearing his voice or feeling his touch, was too much to bear. She had fallen in love with Tarun, had allowed herself to believe that they could find a way out of this nightmare together. But now... now she was alone, and the future seemed bleak and uncertain. Every plan, every promise they had made to each other felt like ashes in her mouth. The world had closed in on her, leaving her adrift in a sea of regret.

The night dragged on, each hour stretching into eternity as Priya sat by the cold hearth, her mind racing with thoughts of Tarun. Where was he? What were they doing to him? Would she ever see him again? The silence of the house pressed down on her, suffocating in its emptiness. She had never felt so alone.

Doubt gnawed at her, and the guilt weighed heavily on her chest. What if she had done the wrong thing? What if she had only delivered Tarun into the clutches of the government? She had tried to protect him, to keep him safe, but had she only made things worse? The questions circled in her mind, relentless and unforgiving. She had promised him that they would fight this together, but in the end, she had failed. She had let him down, and now he was paying the price.

As the hours passed and the darkness outside deepened, Priya's thoughts turned to the villagers. The people of Nagra had suffered for so long under the weight of the government's experiments, and now Tarun had been caught in that same web of fear and control. She couldn't let his capture be in vain—couldn't let the government continue their cruel work. The villagers deserved better. Tarun deserved better.

But what could she do? She was just one person, a small cog in a much larger machine. She had no power to fight back, no way to rescue Tarun from the clutches of the government. All she had were her wits and her knowledge of the village... and the hope that somehow, she could find a way to save him. She had to try. For Tarun's sake. For the villagers' sake. She couldn't let the government continue their experiments unchecked. She couldn't let Tarun's sacrifice be for nothing.

As the cold night wore on, Priya made a silent vow to herself. She wouldn't let Tarun vanish into the shadows of the government's experiments. She would find a way to bring him back, no matter the cost. She had to believe that there was still hope, that she could still save him. The alternative was too painful to consider. She couldn't lose him—not now, not when they had come so far.

But as the night deepened and the village grew quiet, the doubts crept back into her mind. What if it was already too late? What if Tarun was gone, lost to the same fate that had claimed so many others in Nagra? The thought sent a shiver down her spine, and for a moment, she was paralyzed by fear. She couldn't bear the idea of never seeing him again, of never having the chance to tell him how much he meant to her.

As the first light of dawn began to creep over the mountains, Priya finally rose from her seat by the fire. Her body ached with exhaustion, but her mind was set. She couldn't afford to give in to despair. Tarun needed her, and she couldn't let him down again. She had to find him. She had to save him.

With renewed determination, Priya gathered her strength and set off on her journey. The cold air bit at her skin as she stepped outside, the weight of her task pressing down on her shoulders, but she kept moving forward. She had to find Tarun. She had to bring him back, no matter what it took. And she wouldn't stop until she did.

Days passed in a blur as Priya gathered her strength and prepared for what lay ahead. She knew where Tarun had been taken—back to the very place they had tried to infiltrate. The warehouse. The heart of the government's operation. It was there, hidden beneath the mountains, that they kept their prisoners, their test subjects. And it was there that she would find Tarun.

Her mind was set. She would go back, no matter the danger, no matter the cost. She couldn't live with herself if she didn't at least try to save him. The villagers of Nagra had suffered enough under the weight of the government's cruel experiments, and now Tarun was caught in that same nightmare. She had to free him. She had to.

It was late at night when Priya finally made her move. The moon was high in the sky, casting a pale glow over the village as she slipped through the shadows. She had studied the layout of the warehouse, memorized every detail, every entrance and exit. She knew how to get in, how to avoid detection. But even with all her preparation, fear gnawed at her insides. She was going up against forces far larger than herself—forces that could crush her without a second thought.

But she couldn't think about that now. She had to stay focused. She had to find Tarun.

The path to the warehouse was treacherous, winding through steep hills and dense forest. The air was cold, and the ground was slick with moisture from the recent rains. Every step was a risk, every movement carefully calculated to avoid detection. But Priya knew these mountains well. She knew the hidden routes, the secret paths that the government didn't. And so she pressed on, her heart pounding in her chest as she approached the warehouse.

When she finally reached the building, she crouched low in the shadows, her eyes scanning the perimeter. The warehouse was as she remembered it—dark, crumbling, and ominous. But this time, it was different. This time, Tarun was inside, trapped in the belly of the beast. And she had to get him out.

Taking a deep breath, Priya moved swiftly toward the entrance, her footsteps silent on the cold ground. She reached the door and carefully pushed it open, slipping inside without a sound. The air inside the warehouse was stale and oppressive, the walls closing in around her as she moved through the dimly lit corridors. Her heart raced in her chest, every nerve on high alert.

She made her way deeper into the building, following the layout she had memorized. The corridors twisted and turned, leading her deeper into the heart of the facility. She passed empty rooms, abandoned equipment, and the occasional flickering light. But she didn't stop. She couldn't stop. Tarun was close—she could feel it.

Finally, after what felt like an eternity, she reached the room where Tarun was being held. She paused outside the door, her breath catching in her throat as she listened for any sign of movement. The room was quiet—too quiet. But she knew he was in there. She could feel his presence, even through the thick walls.

With a deep breath, Priya pushed the door open and stepped inside.

The room was small and dimly lit, the air thick with the scent of sweat and fear. Tarun was there, bound to a chair in the center of the room, his head slumped forward. His clothes were dirty and torn, his face bruised and battered. But he was alive.

"Tarun," Priya whispered, rushing to his side. She knelt beside him, her hands trembling as she reached for the ropes that bound him.

Tarun stirred at the sound of her voice, lifting his head to look at her. His eyes were filled with pain, but there was a spark of recognition in them—a spark of hope.

"Priya," he rasped, his voice weak but steady. "You... you came back."

"Of course I did," Priya whispered, her voice choked with emotion. "I couldn't leave you here. I couldn't..."

She worked quickly to untie the ropes that bound him, her fingers trembling with urgency. But before she could finish, the door behind them slammed open, and a figure stepped into the room.

"Stop right there," the voice commanded, cold and authoritative.

Priya froze, her heart racing as she turned to face the figure. It was a government official, his face hidden in the shadows, but his presence unmistakable. He held a gun in his hand,

pointed directly at her.

For a moment, time seemed to stand still. Priya's mind raced, her thoughts a whirlwind of fear and desperation. But she couldn't let this be the end. She couldn't let Tarun be taken from her again.

With a sudden burst of adrenaline, Priya lunged toward the official, her hand reaching for the gun tucked into her waistband—a locally made weapon she had acquired in secret. The official was caught off guard, his eyes widening in surprise as Priya raised the gun and fired.

The shot echoed through the room, deafening in the confined space. The official staggered back, clutching his chest as he fell to the ground.

Priya didn't waste a second. She turned back to Tarun, her hands working frantically to finish untying him. "Come on," she urged. "We have to go. Now."

Tarun nodded weakly, his strength slowly returning as Priya freed him from the ropes. He stood up, wincing in pain but determined. Together, they moved toward the door, their hearts pounding in unison.

But as they stepped into the corridor, they were met with a group of officials—more of them, armed and ready for a fight.

The battle that followed was fierce and chaotic. Priya and Tarun fought with everything they had, their movements fueled by desperation and determination. The officials had the advantage of numbers, but Priya and Tarun had the advantage of surprise. They moved quickly, taking out one official after another, their bodies moving in perfect sync.

But then, in the midst of the chaos, a shot rang out—a single, sharp crack that pierced the air.

Priya didn't see the bullet coming. She didn't even feel it at first. But when she looked down, she saw the blood spreading across her chest, the warm, sticky liquid staining her clothes.

She had been hit.

Tarun's eyes widened in horror as he watched Priya stagger backward, her body swaying as she struggled to stay on her feet. "Priya!" he shouted, rushing to her side.

But it was too late. Priya's legs gave out beneath her, and she collapsed into Tarun's arms, her breath coming in shallow gasps. The world around her began to blur, the sounds of the battle fading into the background as she looked up at Tarun.

"I'm sorry," she whispered, her voice barely audible. "I'm so sorry..."

"Don't talk like that," Tarun said urgently, his voice thick with emotion. "You're going to be fine. You're going to be okay."

But Priya knew the truth. She could feel her life slipping away, the darkness closing in around her. She had done what was right. She had saved Tarun. And that was enough.

A soft smile touched her lips as she looked up at him one last time. "I love you," she whispered, her voice a faint echo of the wind.

And then, as the world around her faded into nothingness, Priya closed her eyes and let go.

Tarun's world shattered as Priya's body went limp in his arms. The pain in his chest was unbearable, a physical ache that threatened to tear him apart. But there was no time to grieve—not yet. The battle wasn't over.

With a fierce cry, Tarun rose to his feet, his eyes blazing with fury. He fought with everything he had, every punch, every kick fueled by the pain of losing Priya. The officials were caught off guard by his sudden ferocity, and one by one, they fell before him.

Finally, when the last official was down, Tarun turned to the head of the operation—the man in charge. He grabbed him by the collar, dragging him to his feet and slamming him against the wall.

"Tell your men to put their weapons down," Tarun growled, his voice filled with a dangerous calm. "Or I swear, I'll end you right here."

The man's eyes widened in fear, and he quickly barked out the order. The remaining officials lowered their weapons, their faces pale with shock.

Tarun didn't waste any time. He destroyed the control room, tearing apart the equipment that had been used to manipulate the villagers' minds. He smashed the monitors, ripped out the wires, and watched as the sparks flew and the screens went dark.

And then, as the final piece of machinery fell apart, Tarun heard the sound of footsteps behind him. He turned to see the villagers of Nagra pouring into the building, their faces filled with determination and resolve. They had followed Priya's lead, and now they were here to finish what she had started.

Together, they destroyed everything—every piece of equipment, every control panel, every trace of the government's experiments. They tore down the walls, set fire to the rooms, and watched as the building burned.

And when it was all over, when the warehouse was nothing more than a pile of ashes and rubble, Tarun stood in the wreckage, his heart heavy with both victory and loss.

Priya was gone. She had sacrificed everything to save him, to save the village. And now, as the smoke rose into the sky, Tarun vowed to honor her memory. He would continue the fight, continue to protect the village that she had given her life for.

But as the first light of dawn began to break over the mountains, casting a golden glow over the village of Nagra, Tarun couldn't help but feel the weight of his loss. Priya had been his strength, his hope, his love. And now, she was gone.

But she had saved him. She had saved them all.

And that was a victory worth fighting for.

Chapter 8: Echoes of Her Love

The world felt hollow as Tarun returned to Priya's small home, now silent and empty. The fight was over, the government's control shattered, but victory tasted bitter in his mouth. The weight of Priya's sacrifice pressed down on him, a burden he wasn't sure he could carry. She had been the reason he had fought so hard, the reason he had held onto hope when everything seemed lost. And now, she was gone.

The village of Nagra had gone quiet again, the fires that had burned in the wake of their rebellion now smoldering to ash. The people moved about in a daze, free but wounded by the battle that had claimed so much. And yet, none of them had lost as much as Tarun. None of them had lost Priya.

As he stepped into the house, a profound stillness greeted him. It was as though the air itself had been drained of life. Every corner of the house seemed to echo with memories of her, each shadow a reminder of what he had lost. He had spent so many moments here with her, in the quiet sanctuary of this small space where they had planned, hoped, and dreamed. But now, it felt like a tomb—a place where only ghosts lingered.

Tarun wandered through the rooms, his footsteps heavy, searching for something—anything—that could give him comfort. His eyes scanned the familiar surroundings, taking in the simple furniture, the soft curtains that fluttered in the breeze, the small trinkets that Priya had collected over the years. Everything was just as she had left it, untouched by the chaos outside. Yet all he found was the suffocating silence of her absence.

He moved from room to room, his heart aching with every step. Her presence lingered in every object, every detail. In the kitchen, he could almost see her preparing tea, her hands moving gracefully as she poured it into two cups. In the living room, he imagined her sitting by the window, her gaze lost in thought as she watched the world outside. And in the bedroom...

In the bedroom, where the bed lay unmade as if she had just stepped out for a moment, Tarun's breath caught in his throat. The room was small, with soft light filtering through the window, casting gentle shadows on the walls. It was here that she had rested, where she had found brief moments of peace amidst the turmoil of their lives.

Tarun hesitated before stepping inside, his heart pounding with an unbearable sense of finality. He approached the bed, his fingers brushing against the blanket that still held the faint scent of her perfume. He wanted to feel close to her, to hold on to some piece of her that hadn't been taken away. But all he found was the emptiness that her absence left behind.

And then, as he sat on the edge of the bed, something caught his eye—a small, folded note tucked beneath the pillow where she used to rest her head.

His breath stilled as he reached for it, his fingers trembling. He recognized Priya's delicate handwriting on the paper, the familiar curve of each letter that he had seen in the notes she had left him during their time together. The sight of it was both a comfort and a dagger to his heart.

With shaking hands, Tarun unfolded the note, his heart pounding in his chest as he prepared himself for whatever words Priya had left behind. He sank onto the edge of the bed, his hands trembling as he began to read.

The note was a confession, an outpouring of regret and love. Every word cut deeper than the last, revealing the truth that Priya had kept hidden from him for so long. As he read, the world seemed to blur around him, leaving only her words and the pain that accompanied them.

Tarun,

If you're reading this, then I'm already gone. I wish I could have told you everything sooner, but I was a coward. I was afraid—afraid of what you would think of me, afraid of losing you. But now, I have nothing left to lose.

I need you to know the truth. I've been hiding something from you, something terrible. I was never just the village schoolteacher you thought I was. I worked for the government. I was their eyes in Nagra, their agent sent to watch over the people and ensure they didn't step out of line. My task was to monitor the villagers, to report any signs of rebellion or resistance to the Mind-Wave project.

And when you arrived in Nagra, I was assigned to watch you too. I was ordered to keep an eye on you, to ensure that you didn't uncover the truth. That's how it all started. I was supposed to be your enemy.

Tarun's hands clenched around the paper as he read her words, his heart aching with every sentence. The betrayal stung deep, cutting through the love he had held for her. She had been working for the very people they had fought against, the very people who had caused so much suffering in Nagra. But as he continued reading, the pain of betrayal gave way to something deeper—something that pulled him back into the love he had shared with her.

But then something happened that I never expected. I got to know you. And the more I knew you, the more I realized that I couldn't do what they asked of me. I couldn't betray you, not after seeing the kindness in your heart, the strength in your spirit. But I was trapped, Tarun. I was caught between my duty and my love for you, and I didn't know how to escape.

I watched you talk to Ravi. I knew what he was telling you, and I was terrified. I was terrified that you would uncover the truth, that you would expose the government's secrets. And so, I made a terrible choice. I decided to lead you into the hands of the officials. I told myself it was the only way to keep you safe—to stop you from going too far and getting yourself killed.

Tarun's heart twisted with each word, the weight of her confession pressing down on him. She had betrayed him—led him straight into the hands of the very people they had been fighting against. But as he read on, he could see the depth of her regret, the agony she had carried with her as she tried to navigate the impossible choices before her.

But when I handed you over to them, something inside me broke. I realized that I had made the wrong choice, that I had betrayed the only person who had ever truly cared for me. And I knew that I had to make it right, no matter the cost. That's why I came back for you. That's why I fought to save you, even though I knew it would be the end for me.

I didn't deserve your love, Tarun. I was a coward, and I made so many mistakes. But I loved you. I loved you more than I ever thought possible, and I would do anything to protect you—even if it meant sacrificing my own life.

If I'm gone, then I want you to know that I'm at peace. I'm at peace because I know that you're safe, that you're free. And that's all I ever wanted—for you to be free.

Maybe in another life, we'll find each other again. Maybe then, I'll be brave enough to tell you the truth from the beginning. But until then, I'll carry your love with me, wherever I go.

Goodbye, Tarun. I'm sorry for everything. But above all, I'm sorry that I didn't get to spend more time with you. I hope you can forgive me.

Yours always,

Priya

The note, stained with dried tears, slipped from Tarun's fingers as he sat in stunned silence. Her words echoed in his mind, a haunting melody of love, regret, and sacrifice. She had been torn between her duty and her love for him, and in the end, she had chosen to save him, even if it meant giving up her own life.

Tarun's mind reeled, caught between the agony of her loss and the bittersweet promise of reunion. He could still feel her presence in the room, a lingering warmth that wrapped around him like a final embrace. The room was filled with her scent, her energy, her love. And yet, she was gone—taken from him by the very forces they had fought against.

He whispered her name into the night, each breath a plea for the peace that eluded him. "Priya..."

But there was no answer. Only the cold silence of the empty house, the shadows that lingered in every corner, and the weight of her sacrifice that pressed down on his chest.

Tarun knew he would never fully heal from the loss. Priya had been the light in his life, the one who had given him hope when everything seemed lost. And now that light had gone out, leaving him adrift in a world that felt colder and darker than ever before.

But even in his grief, Tarun knew that he couldn't let her sacrifice be in vain. She had given him back his life, and he owed it to her to live, to protect the village, to ensure that no one else would suffer as they had. He had to carry on, not just for himself, but for Priya—for the love they had shared, for the promise she had made to him in her final moments.

He stood up from the bed, the note still clutched in his hand. The world outside was quiet, the village of Nagra shrouded in the soft light of dawn. The battles they had fought, the horrors they had endured, were behind them now. But the scars remained, etched into the very fabric of the village.

Tarun walked to the window, his gaze drifting out over the mountains that loomed in the distance. The sun was beginning to rise, casting a golden glow over the peaks and valleys. It was a new day—a new beginning. And yet, it was a day that Priya would never see.

Tears welled in his eyes as he thought of her—of the love they had shared, of the future they had dreamed of but would never have. But even in his sorrow, there was a quiet strength that began to grow within him. He would carry her memory with him, her love, her sacrifice. And he would use that strength to protect the village she had given her life for.

As the sun climbed higher into the sky, Tarun made a silent vow. He would honor Priya's memory. He would protect the people of Nagra, ensure that the government's experiments would never return. He would live the life she had fought so hard to give him. And in doing so, he would keep her spirit alive.

For Priya. For the love they had shared. For the promise of reunion in another life.

Chapter 9: Melodies of the Forgotten

The couple sat on the old wooden bench, mesmerized by the tale the old man had spun. Tarun's voice had been soft but steady, filled with the weight of years and emotions too vast to be contained in mere words. As the story unfolded, they were drawn into a world long past, a world shaped by love, loss, and sacrifice. Each word seemed to linger in the air, heavy with meaning, painting vivid images in their minds of a time and place they could only imagine.

They didn't know that this story wasn't just a tale—it was Tarun's own life, a life that had been shaped by forces beyond his control. Every moment of joy, every heartache, every decision that had led him to where he was now had been woven into the fabric of his story. And now, sitting beside this young couple, he had shared it with them, offering them a glimpse into the life he had lived, and the love he had lost.

When the story ended, the couple remained still, the weight of his words hanging in the air between them. The sun had dipped below the horizon, leaving behind the soft hues of twilight that bathed the village of Nagra in a gentle glow. The air was cool, carrying with it the scent of pine and earth, and the world seemed to hold its breath, as if waiting for something to happen.

The couple turned to thank him, to ask him more about his life, to understand the depth of the emotions he had so eloquently expressed. But when they looked toward the bench where Tarun had been sitting, they found it empty. The old man was gone, as though he had never been there at all.

Confused, they looked around, searching for any sign of him. The village was quiet, the streets empty, and the only sound was the rustling of the trees in the evening breeze. It was as if Tarun had vanished into the air, leaving behind only the faintest trace of his presence. They called out his name, their voices echoing in the stillness, but there was no answer. Only silence.

And then, just as they were about to give up and leave, they heard it—a soft, sorrowful melody that drifted on the wind. It was distant but unmistakable, the same melody they had heard before, the one that had accompanied Tarun's story:

"Through every breath, I still feel you near,
Yet every step I take is shadowed by the tear..."

The couple stood there, listening to the haunting melody as it floated through the air, carried by the wind like a whispered secret. It was as if the song itself was alive, moving through the village, winding through the trees and along the riverbanks, touching everything in its path. They could feel the old man's presence in the music, a lingering echo of the love that had once filled his life.

For a long time, they remained where they were, staring into the fading light of twilight, their hearts heavy with the story they had just heard. There was a sadness in the air, a deep sense of loss that seemed to permeate everything around them. And yet, there was also something else—something beautiful and eternal, like the melody that continued to play on the wind.

They couldn't shake the feeling that they had just brushed against something otherworldly, something that transcended time and space. Tarun's story wasn't just a tale of love and loss—it was a living presence, a force that lingered in the village of Nagra long after the world had moved on. The melody echoed in their minds, and they knew that they would carry it with them for the rest of their lives.

When they finally left Nagra, it was with a sense of wonder and sadness that they couldn't quite explain. They had come to the village seeking peace and beauty, but they had found something much deeper—an ancient love story that still lived in the hearts of those who had known it. Tarun's love, though lost to time, had not faded. It lingered in the village, in the wind, in the river, in the very earth beneath their feet.

As they walked away, they glanced back at the bench where the old man had sat. It was empty now, but in their minds, they could still see him there, telling his story, his eyes filled with the weight of years and the memory of a love that had never truly left him.

The village of Nagra, wrapped in its quiet magic, held onto its secrets, and the love story that had shaped its history continued to whisper through the air, a reminder that some melodies never truly fade. The couple knew that they had been touched by something extraordinary, something that would stay with them forever.

And as they left Nagra behind, they carried with them the echoes of a lost melody—a love that had transcended time, a love that would endure long after the world had forgotten Tarun's name.

Epilogue

Years had passed since the young couple had visited the village of Nagra, yet the memory of that day lingered with them like a dream that refused to fade. They often spoke of the old man they had met, of the haunting melody that had drifted through the air, and of the love story he had shared—a love so profound, it had transcended time itself. It was a story that had stayed with them, shaping the way they viewed the world, love, and loss.

But time, as it always does, moved forward. Seasons changed, and the world outside Nagra continued on, unaware of the whispers that still lingered in the quiet village. Yet, for those who knew where to listen, the echoes of that love story never truly disappeared.

In the village square, beneath the same old tree, the worn wooden bench remained. The villagers still passed by it, some with a glance of recognition, others with a quiet nod, but no one sat there for long. It was as though the bench still held the presence of the man who had once sat there, waiting for something—or someone.

And though Tarun was no longer there in body, his spirit seemed to linger in the air. The melody he had sung, that haunting tune of love and loss, still floated through the village from time to time. It would catch on the wind, softly brushing against the ears of those who passed by, a gentle reminder that some loves never truly die.

The river still whispered its secrets, winding its way through the village with a timeless grace. The ancient trees still stood tall, their branches reaching for the sky as if they could touch the very essence of the past. And the wind—always the wind—carried whispers through the mountains, whispers of an endless love that had once been, and still was.

One day, years after their visit, the couple returned to Nagra. They were older now, the rush of youth replaced by a quieter understanding of life. The village seemed the same, yet different—still beautiful, still serene, but with an air of mystery that hadn't faded. They walked through the familiar streets, memories rising with every step, until they found themselves back at the square.

The bench was empty, just as it had been that day, but the air around it was alive with the same quiet magic. As they stood there, side by side, the breeze shifted, and once again, they heard it—the melody that had haunted them for so long:

"Through every breath, I still feel you near,
Yet every step I take is shadowed by the tear..."

The sound was soft, almost imperceptible, but it carried the weight of something eternal. The couple smiled at each other, their hearts warmed by the memory of the old man and his story. They knew, as they had known all those years ago, that Nagra held something special—something timeless.

As they walked away, hand in hand, they couldn't help but glance back one last time. The village square, the bench, the old tree—they all remained, suspended in time, a testament to a love that had endured beyond life itself.

And somewhere, in the quiet corners of the village, in the rustling of the trees and the whispers of the wind, Tarun's love story continued to live on. It was no longer just his—it belonged to the village, to the mountains, to the world. It was a love that had touched the lives of those who heard it, and would continue to do so for generations to come.

For some loves never truly fade. They linger, like a whisper, carried on the wind, forever a part of the places and people they touched.

About the Author

Biswajit Paria is a storyteller who weaves tales that delve deep into the heart of human emotions, blending love, loss, and the mysteries of life with a poetic touch. With a unique voice and a vivid imagination, Biswajit crafts stories that linger in the minds of readers long after the last page is turned. His narratives often explore the timeless themes of relationships, the passage of time, and the echoes of the past, bringing together elements of nature and nostalgia in ways that resonate deeply with his audience.

Biswajit Paria draws inspiration from the world around him. Whether it's the quiet beauty of a village nestled in the mountains or the haunting whispers of a forgotten love story, he infuses his work with a sense of place that is as alive as the characters he creates.

In **"Whispers of an Endless Love,"** Biswajit explores the endurance of love beyond life's boundaries, set against the backdrop of the hauntingly beautiful village of Nagra. Through his lyrical prose and compelling storytelling, he invites readers to journey with him into a world where love transcends time and whispers linger on the wind.

When he's not writing, Biswajit enjoys exploring the hidden corners of nature, where he often finds inspiration for his stories. His connection to the natural world and his deep curiosity about life's mysteries continue to shape his work, making him a distinctive voice in contemporary fiction.

Don't miss out!

Visit the website below and you can sign up to receive emails whenever Biswajit Paria publishes a new book. There's no charge and no obligation.

https://books2read.com/r/B-A-CWOKC-XXXYE

BOOKS2READ

Connecting independent readers to independent writers.

Also by Biswajit Paria

A Letter Never Delivered
Whispers of an Endless Love